The Smallest Horse in the World

by

Jeremy Strong

Illustrated by Scoular Anderson

D0227038

STAFFORDSHIRE LIBRARIES ARTS AND ARCHIVES	
38014039302630	
PET	19-May-05
CF	£4.99
PENK	

You do not need to read this page – just get on with the book!

First published in 2005 in Great Britain by
Barrington Stoke Ltd, Sandeman House, Trunk's Close,
55 High Street, Edinburgh EH1 1SR
www.barringtonstoke.co.uk

Copyright © 2005 Jeremy Strong
Illustrations © Scoular Anderson

The moral right of the author has been asserted in accordance with the Copyright, Designs and Patents Act 1988

ISBN 1-842993-21-6

Printed in Great Britain by Bell & Bain Ltd

Meet The Author – Jeremy Strong

What is your favourite animal?

A cat

What is your favourite boy's name?

Magnus Pinchbottom

What is your favourite girl's name?

Wobbly Wendy

What is your favourite food?

Chicken Kiev (I love garlic)

What is your favourite music?

Soft

What is your favourite hobby?

Sleeping

Meet The Illustrator – Scoular Anderson

What is your favourite animal?

Humorous dogs

What is your favourite boy's name?

Orlando

What is your favourite girl's name?

Esmerelda

What is your favourite food?

Garlicky, tomatoey pasta

What is your favourite music?

Big orchestras

What is your favourite hobby?

Long walks

This is for Bella who likes animals
(and strawberries) of all sizes

Contents

Chapter 1
Swan

Bella had a problem with the new girl in her class. She was called Swan. *What a lovely name for a girl,* Bella thought. But the problem was this. Swan wasn't very nice and Bella didn't like her.

Swan hadn't been at the school long and she was hard to like. She was a show-off. She was rude and loud and big and bossy. She was always telling everyone how rich her parents were.

"They've got millions," she said on her first day at school.

"They've got billions," she said on the second day. By the end of the week Swan's parents had squillions. Bella got the feeling that Swan *might* be lying.

"You're making it all up – about your parents being so rich," Bella said, in front of everyone.

Swan stopped dead and stared at Bella. Bella could see she was very angry. Swan stuck her hands on her hips, stepped in front of Bella and stood so close they were almost touching.

"I am NOT making it up," Swan snarled. "My parents are rich, rich, rich. They've got a big posh car *and* a Ferrari and a helicopter. So there." Swan stuck out her tongue.

Bella stepped back. Swan was a big girl, and Bella wasn't. "Well," Bella went on, "I don't believe you. And you've got a silly name."

This wasn't true at all. Bella wished she hadn't said it, but she had, and now it was too late. In fact, she loved the name. She wished she was called Swan. Bella was angry that a big, lumpy girl could be given such a lovely name.

"Well, just listen to you," snapped Swan. "I've got a funny name, have I? What about yours, Belly?" The other children started to laugh.

"Belly!" they giggled.

"Smelly Belly!" Swan shouted with glee, and everyone laughed some more.

Bella felt her face go hot. She felt angry and ashamed. She couldn't think of anything clever to say. She stood there for a few seconds, listening to everyone laughing. Then she turned round and ran off.

"Jelly Belly!" Swan yelled after her.

For the rest of the school day Bella stayed as far away from Swan as she could. At the end of the afternoon she went out to Mum's car and got in quickly. She didn't say anything all the way home. Mum could see something was wrong but she didn't ask what it was. Ever since Bella's mum and dad had split up Bella had been a bit quiet.

When they got home Bella ran to her room and lay on the bed, staring up at the ceiling. Then she stared at the floor. After that, she stared at the wall. *School was horrible*, she thought. *And Swan was more than horrible. Swan was ...?* What was she? She was ten times horrible. A hundred, a thousand, a million times horrible.

Bella gazed at the wall and she looked over to the picture by her little desk. She loved that picture. She often tried to think what it would be like if she was inside the picture. Most of all she liked to do this when she was upset. The painting was of a wonderful white horse, galloping through waves that crashed onto a golden beach. You could see the sea-spray coming up from the horse's hooves. You could see the sea wind blowing the horse's mane. You could almost feel the spray from the waves and smell the salty air.

Bella went and stood in front of the picture. She wanted to get as close to it as she could and see every little detail. Standing there, she thought she could *feel* the breeze blowing off the sea and right out through the glass.

She stretched up and lifted the painting off the wall. She didn't know it was so heavy.

In fact, the picture was so heavy that she dropped it. It crashed onto her desk. *BANG!*

The frame split apart. The glass broke into tiny splinters.

But that was not all. As the picture came apart, water and sand poured onto Bella's desk, spread across to the edge and dribbled on to the carpet.

And the wonderful white horse stood there, on her desk, shaking its mane and whinnying softly. A white horse, perfect in every detail, except that it was only the size of a small kitten.

Chapter 2
Astra

Bella was amazed – just as you would be if a real horse suddenly fell out of a picture and landed on your desk. She was even more amazed when the horse looked up at her and spoke.

"Have you seen Rufus?" The horse's voice was soft and sweet, a bit like Bella's mum's voice, when she was in a good mood.

"Rufus?" Bella asked.

"He's my rider," the horse explained. "I've been looking and looking. We got split up in the battle. I'm not sure what happened." The horse looked sad. "Maybe he was killed," the little horse went on. "I hope not. We've been together for years. He's a good rider and a good master, too."

The horse stopped and looked around the room. She saw at once she was somewhere quite different from before and she gave a little whinny of surprise. Bella was rather surprised herself.

"This is very strange," they both said together, then looked at each other shyly. Bella smiled and she thought the horse smiled too. Could horses smile? Bella thought so. Bella knew so.

"I'm called Astra," said the horse.

“And my name’s Bella. This is my bedroom.”

“Ah.” The horse nodded and then gave a long sigh. “Oh dear,” she said softly. “Now I am well and truly lost. You see how small I am in your world? I must get back into the world I came from. Then I shall be the right size and I might be able to find my master, Rufus. But all the time I’m here, like this, I have no chance.”

Bella looked down at the floor, where the last few drops of seawater were soaking into the sand that had dropped onto the carpet. “I can’t put the picture back together,” she whispered. “I’m so sorry.”

“Then I have lost him forever,” said Astra with a sigh, hanging her head.

Bella didn’t know what to say. But she saw the mess on the floor and she knew she had to tidy up. If Astra was going to stay in her bedroom, then should she tell Mum? She went to the door. What would Mum say? Bella didn't know if Mum would believe that there was a kitten-sized horse in her room. In fact, she knew she wouldn't! Bella could hardly believe it herself.

She thought she'd better get a dustpan and brush and clear up the sand and glass and bits of broken picture frame. Yes, that was the first thing to do. She looked back at Astra, who was wandering around the books and pens on Bella's desk. Then Astra lifted her tail.

"No!" cried Bella, but it was too late. Astra did what horses do, even very small horses. Now Bella had horse poo to clean up, too. Perhaps keeping a horse in her bedroom was not going to be as brilliant as she had thought.

Chapter 3

No roses in the bedroom, please

Bella learned a lot of things about Astra that evening. She found out that Astra liked eating straw and sugar lumps and apples. Bella also found Astra chewing all her felt-tip pens – the ones with the fruity smells. The felt-tips left coloured marks all over Astra's muzzle and lips. Soon she became a horse with a polka-dot mouth. Bella had to wash her clean.

After that, Bella put Astra on the floor where she thought the horse couldn't do much harm. Fat chance! Astra loved the straw rug beside Bella's bed. She ate a big lump off the corner before Bella even saw what was happening, and then lifted her tail again. Bella seemed to spend the whole evening rushing to and fro with the dustpan and brush.

"Where are you going?" asked Mum.

"I spilled something," Bella shouted as she dashed back upstairs. Her room smelt awful. "Oh yuk," she muttered and ran downstairs once more.

"Where are you going?" asked Mum, again.

"I forgot something," Bella shouted as she dashed back upstairs with a can of air-freshener. Astra was galloping round and round the little bedroom.

"What's that noise?" Mum called up the stairs.

"I'm practising tap-dancing," Bella called back.

"But you don't do tap-dancing, darling."

"That's why I'm practising," Bella answered in a bright voice. She hissed at Astra, "Can't you make a bit less noise when you gallop? I've got to keep you a secret. If Mum finds out she'll ... I don't know! She'll probably send you to the Very Small Horse Rescue Farm or something," Bella giggled. It was all very silly, and great fun.

At last Astra settled down. Bella made the horse a stable for the night in the front room of her old dolls' house. She put in some straw she had taken from the rabbit's hutch and some bits of carrot too. "And if you want to go, please go in the corner," she told the horse.

"If I want to go? What do you mean?" asked Astra.

"You know – *go*."

"I can't *go*. You've shut the door," Astra said.

"I don't mean that kind of go. I mean **go**."

The horse was very puzzled by now. "What kind of go is **go**?" she asked. Bella leaned out of her bed, put her mouth very close to Astra's flicking ears and whispered.

"Oh!" said Astra, with surprise. "But horse poo's supposed to be very good for growing roses."

"Roses don't grow in my bedroom," Bella pointed out.

"They might if I *go* lots," Astra said helpfully.

"NO!" said Bella firmly. "They won't! Roses grow outside and not in bedrooms. Now please go to sleep and stop making things difficult."

For a little while everything was quiet. Then Astra spoke. "Do you think I shall ever find Rufus?"

"I hope so," Bella replied sleepily, even though she had no idea how to help, or what to do, or where to start.

"What will happen tomorrow?" asked Astra.

Bella's eyes snapped open. Tomorrow! Now that was a good question. She had school the next day. Mum would be out at work so that would be OK, but would Astra be safe, left alone in the house?

Chapter 4
More trouble with Swan

In the morning Bella was glad to find that Astra had spent the whole night asleep and there was no more mess. The poor horse must have been worn out after tumbling from the picture. Bella gazed down at the sleepy animal and thought that she had never seen such a perfect creature. She wanted badly to stay with Astra, but she had to have breakfast with Mum and go to school.

Sitting still at the table and eating her cornflakes was probably the hardest thing that Bella had done for ages and ages. She was longing to tell Mum about Astra, but every time she looked at Mum she felt she just couldn't. Mum wouldn't believe her. And if Mum ever did find Astra, Bella knew she would say there was no way Bella could keep a mini-horse in her bedroom – most of all one that did poos all over the place.

So Bella tried to keep still and eat her breakfast as fast as she could. Mum noticed, of course.

"You're in a hurry today," she said. "Are you looking forward to school?"

"Yes!" Bella said happily. She gave a big pretend smile, but inside her heart had started to thump. Mum's words had made her remember that someone was waiting for her at school. Swan. Swan and all those children who had laughed at her yesterday.

Bella made sure Astra was safe in her room and told the horse to be good.

"I'm always good," said Astra crossly. "I only do what all horses do."

"Horses don't eat felt-tips," Bella muttered.

"But they smelt so nice," Astra replied.

Bella wagged a finger. "Be good!" She shut the door.

At school Swan was there as always, strutting round the playground. "My dad's going to buy us a swimming pool," she told everyone. "It's going to have water slides and real fish, too."

The children around her gasped. "Wow!"

"Yeah, and, AND it's going to have not just fish, but dolphins as well."

"That is so cool!" everyone cried. "Dolphins!"

"Yeah," nodded Swan smugly. "Dolphins and hippos."

Bella couldn't believe her ears. All the other children seemed to think this was true. It couldn't be. It was crazy. Something inside her snapped.

"That's rubbish," said Bella.

"Oh look, it's Smelly Belly again," sneered Swan. "It's not rubbish. We're getting a swimming pool."

"You're never going to have dolphins and hippos. You're just making things up. I don't think your parents are rich at all. I don't think you've got posh cars or anything."

Swan was stunned, and very angry. She seemed to swell up and get even bigger. Her face went purple. “Oh, yes we are. We’re richer than all of you lot put together! My dad’s always buying us stuff. You should have been at my house last night. My dad got me a pony.”

“No, he didn’t!” shouted Bella.

“He did! And he’s brown with a white star on his forehead.”

The two girls looked hard at each other until Bella couldn’t stand it any longer. “Well, I don’t care if he did, because I’ve got my own horse at home, so there.”

The other children stopped and stared at her. They had known Bella for ages. “No, you haven’t, Bella. You haven’t got a horse.”

“Yes, I have.”

"You can't have one," said Swan, "because girls don't ride horses, they ride ponies."

"It's a horse," Bella insisted.

"OK," sneered Swan. "Prove it. Bring your horse to school tomorrow."

For the first time in ages Bella smiled. Her heart slowed down and she felt a lovely calm pass through her body. "All right," she said, "I will. And Swan can bring us her pony too."

Bella turned away and walked off, but as she turned she saw Swan's face and in Swan's eyes she saw ... WILD PANIC.

Chapter 5
Astra goes to school

"Don't you think the house smells a bit?" asked Mum, as she opened the front door that evening.

"Not really," Bella said but she knew Mum was right.

"It does. It smells like a stable in here. How long is it since you cleaned out the rabbit's hutch?"

"Oh! Yes, it could be that," said Bella quickly. "I'll clean it this evening." Then she rushed upstairs and slowly opened her bedroom door. As soon as she did Astra came galloping across the room towards her – clump, clumpety-clump, clump.

"Ssh!" Bella warned. "Mum will hear you."

"Did you find Rufus?" asked Astra. "Did you find him?"

Bella shook her head. "I'm sorry. I don't even know where to start looking." She sat down on her bed. "Mum says the house smells like a stable, and it does, too."

"I like it," Astra said happily.

"That's because you're a horse. It's not the kind of smell humans like."

"Rufus never minded."

Bella gazed at the little horse. She felt she should get to know something more about Rufus and Astra. "Where do you *really* come from?" she asked Astra. "And please stop eating my straw rug."

"We were fighting the Romans," Astra said proudly.

"The Romans? But that was 2,000 years ago!"

"I don't know anything about that. There was a really big battle. I think we were winning and then there was a surprise attack by Roman horsemen. They came from behind us. This chariot suddenly loomed up beside me and I almost had to jump right over it. Rufus fell off my back but I had to keep going. I ran far away from the battle. I went back much later when the battle was over and the Romans had gone. It was horrible. There were so many dead bodies.

But I couldn't find Rufus. That's why I think he must still be alive."

"But he just couldn't be alive now," Bella said gently. "You're talking about something that happened 2,000 years ago. Rufus couldn't be alive now even if he didn't die in the battle."

Astra shook her head and neighed. Her eyes shone. "I'm here," she pointed out. "I'm alive. And I think Rufus is, too. So where do we start looking?"

Bella had to admit that Astra was brave and was not going to give up easily. She thought for a bit. She was going to take Astra to school the next day to show Swan. They might as well begin the hunt for Rufus there. It was as good a place to start as any.

The following morning Bella slipped Astra into her school bag and off they both went. Bella had a good feeling as she set off. She didn't care about Swan any longer. She didn't even care if Swan did bring a real pony to school, but she was pretty sure Swan hadn't got one at all. Bella had Astra in her bag and that was all she needed.

"It's Smelly Jelly Belly!" Swan shouted as soon as she saw Bella in the playground. "Where's your horse? Ha! You haven't got one!" Swan turned to the others. She looked very smug. "Belly hasn't got one! Belly hasn't got one!" she chanted.

"Where's your pony?" Bella asked. "You were supposed to bring *your* pony."

"Well, I couldn't, could I? Dad wouldn't let me. He said you're not allowed ponies at school."

"You haven't got a pony," Bella said softly.

"Have, have, so there. He's called ... Black Beauty."

Bella folded her arms across her chest. "You said your pony was brown."

"Never did!" Swan shouted.

The crowd of children started to mutter. "You did, Swan. Yesterday you said he was brown with a white star on his forehead."

Swan went red. "Well, I forgot. I got in a muddle, that's all. His name's Brown Beauty."

"You haven't got a pony," Bella said again.

"And you haven't got a horse!" yelled Swan.

Bella slowly opened her bag. Everyone was looking at her. She put both her hands into her bag and gently lifted Astra from inside. She put Astra down in the playground. Astra lifted her head. She snorted, pawed the ground and shook her mane. Then she began a little gallop round Bella's feet, enjoying the space and freedom of the playground.

The children just stood there and stared and stared and stared.

"Oh, wow!" breathed one at last. "It's a horse. A real, miniature horse!"

There was a dull thud from nearby. Swan lay crumpled in a heap. She'd fainted from the shock.

Chapter 6
Trouble

Bella ran over to Swan and helped her sit up. "Are you all right?"

"I saw a tiny horse," whispered Swan. "But it's not true, is it? It's some kind of trick."

"It is true. The horse's name is Astra. She fell out of a picture at my house."

Swan tried to smile and stood up slowly. "*My* pony gallops ..." she began, but she didn't finish. Her mouth shut and she gave a long sigh.

Bella was already feeling sorry for Swan. It must feel horrible to do all that bragging and then be found out. Bella began to think that Swan didn't look quite so big after all.

"It's OK," Bella said quietly. "I know you never had a pony."

Swan didn't say a word. They watched Astra galloping round, jumping over the children's feet. The children were laughing and pointing at Astra. Swan sighed again.

"I wish I did have a pony. I wish I had a," Swan's voice dropped to a tiny whisper of a whisper, "dad."

Bella stopped and stared at Swan. She would never have guessed that in a million years. Swan didn't have a dad! "My dad doesn't live at home either," she said, and the two girls turned and looked at each other.

At that moment the bell went and it was time to go into school. Bella called Astra, picked her up and tucked her back in the bag. Everyone wanted to know what to do next.

"You shouldn't bring horses to school," said one girl whose name was Rose. "We'll all get into trouble now."

"You think everything's trouble, Rose," Bella said back. "We just have to keep Astra a secret. You know what teachers are like. They'll take her from us if they find out."

"And make her into dog food," added Martin Blagdon, who was well known for his wild stories. "A very small tin of dog food, because she's a very small horse."

"You're stupid," Swan snapped, almost back to her old self.

"And you're ... umm, bigger than me," squeaked Martin with a grin.

Bella told everyone about Astra's hunt for Rufus. They wanted to know what Rufus looked like. Bella didn't know. She didn't even know what size he was. Suppose Rufus was a small man, just like Astra was a small horse?

"I only know that he was fighting the Romans," she said.

Swan nodded. "Maybe he came from the Iron Age. They fought the Romans," she said. "They wore cloaks and leggings and tunics."

"Yeah, and they all had long hair and big moustaches," Martin added. "Huge moustaches," he went on. "Huge, HUGE moustaches, like great big caterpillars wiggling under their noses."

"Martin!" they all shouted.

Bella tried to make everyone stay calm. "We must try and find Rufus and that means we need to look out for him wherever we are."

"In the classroom," suggested Swan.

"Up the shops," added Rose.

"Down the toilet," Martin said with a grin.

"MARTIN!" they all shouted, and then went into school.

Everything was fine for a while. Astra kept very quiet inside Bella's school bag. But as time went by she became more and more restless. She wanted to get on with the hunt for Rufus. She wanted to get back to the playground where she could run and gallop. Astra gave a little whinny to make Bella notice her, but Bella wasn't listening. Astra whinnied again, more loudly this time.

"Sssh," whispered Bella, and there was silence for a few minutes.

Then – neee-hee-heee-harr!!! Astra was at it again.

The teacher, Mr Frost, leaped from his chair and glared at the class. He scanned each child's face with angry eyes. His eyebrows flicked up and down as they always did when he was cross. When he got to Bella, Mr Frost stopped. He looked hard at her. Bella had one hand in her bag.

"Bella! WHAT are you doing? Bring your bag here at once."

"But I haven't ..."

"Don't argue, girl. I can see you're up to something. Bring your bag here at once."

Chapter 7
Swan wants to be a horse

Bella stood up. She lifted the bag from the back of her chair and began to walk towards Mr Frost. At that same moment another chair scraped across the floor and a child came hurtling forward across the classroom.

"It was me, Mr Frost!" cried Swan. "It was me! I made that funny noise! Neee-hurrr!!!! I was being a horse."

Mr Frost looked at Swan and thought what a very odd girl she was.

"Why?" he asked.

"I like horses," Swan told him. "And I want to be one when I grow up." The class burst out laughing.

"You want to be a horse when you grow up?" repeated Mr Frost.

"Yes. A white one."

Mr Frost gazed at Swan. *What a very strange child,* he thought. "I think you'd better go back and sit down, both of you. Swan, please save your horse noises for the playground."

Bella smiled at Swan as they went back to their seats. It had been a narrow escape. And then, almost as Bella got to her table, the strap of her bag caught on the back of Martin's chair. The bag fell right off her shoulder. It landed on the ground with a heavy thump.

There was a loud, angry neigh from Astra and a moment later she jumped out of the bag. Then she set off at high speed, across the classroom floor, clattering beneath the table legs, jumping over children's feet, and then off and away she went, right out through the door and vanished.

Mr Frost stood up, staring after the horse as it galloped out of the room. "What on earth was that?" he demanded. There was a chorus of replies.

"A dog!"

"A rabbit!"

"A hedgehog!" This came from Martin Blagdon of course.

"A *white* hedgehog?" Mr Frost said crossly.

"So you can't see it when it snows," nodded Martin.

Mr Frost pushed his way past the children. "Stay in class while I go after that animal. If I find that one of you has brought a dog into school then there's going to be real trouble."

The class watched as Mr Frost vanished. They all felt very worried. "We've got to find Astra before he does," Bella hissed.

"I know we're going to get into trouble," moaned Rose.

Swan glared at the girl. “Are you going to help or not?”

Rose nodded. It was less trouble to help find Astra than to argue with Swan. Bella grinned.

The children crept from the classroom and tiptoed into the hall. They spread out, searching everywhere, as quietly as possible. However, they needn’t have bothered to keep quiet because all at once the hall was full of other people shouting.

“There’s a cat in the classroom!” Miss Mousetail came out of her classroom with all her children behind her.

“Help! It’s a badger!” cried Mrs Wood. She stood on her desk and waved a rolled up newspaper. All her class climbed on to their desks too.

"I saw a tiger!" yelled someone from Year 1.

"He needs his eyes testing," muttered Martin Blagdon, which was a bit rich, coming from him.

Then Bella heard the sound she was most dreading. Mr Frost's voice boomed above everyone else.

"Over here!" he bellowed. "It's over here!"

Everyone rushed up the corridor to Mr Frost. Bella and Swan pushed their way through the crowd. Everyone was gazing down at the floor by Mr Frost's big feet. There, right in the middle of the floor was ...

... Phew! At least it wasn't Astra. But it was something Astra had done.

Mr Frost folded his arms and fixed his eyes very firmly on Swan and Bella. He looked very angry and his face was bright red. His eyebrows were leaping about like firecrackers.

"Well?" he growled. "Are you going to explain this?"

Chapter 8
Miss Snow

Bella kept quiet. She didn't know exactly what Mr Frost wanted her to explain.

Swan slipped her hand into Bella's and squeezed it tightly.

"It's that animal that one of you brought in, isn't it?" Mr Frost said. "I know you're in this together. Just what kind of creature is it? I demand to know at once."

Bella chewed her lip. She was beginning to think that Mr Frost's eyebrows would fly right off his face if he wasn't careful. She badly wanted to keep her secret, but she did wish she knew where the little horse was.

"If you won't tell me what this is all about, then you'll have to tell the head teacher," snapped Mr Frost. "Then you can come back here and clean up the floor."

The head teacher, Miss Snow, was a bit more friendly than Mr Frost, but it was not at all nice standing in front of her and getting told off.

"Oh dear," said Miss Snow, when she heard the story. "Oh dear, dear, dear. You can't bring animals into school. Oh no, no, no. Rabbits in the classroom? No, no, no, no."

Swan and Bella wondered how often Miss Snow would go on saying the same thing again and again.

Bella started gazing at the picture behind Miss Snow's head, and the more she looked at it the more she thought … yes, it must be. She nudged Swan and looked up towards the picture. Swan looked up too. Her eyes grew big and she nodded back at Bella.

The painting was of a man standing near the edge of a cliff. He was looking out over a beach and the crashing sea. His cloak billowed in the sea wind and his hand was up by his eyes, as if he was looking for someone, or something.

At that moment Bella noticed something else. Astra.

The little horse was right by Miss Snow's feet, quietly chewing the straw mat on the floor. Bella swallowed hard. She tried to make Astra notice her, but the horse was far too busy eating.

Astra went on quietly munching the mat. Then she found the end of Miss Snow's shoelaces and began to chew those. Bella could hardly bear it. Swan had noticed too. But there was nothing either of them could do. The two girls watched as Astra slowly ate the shoelace. It got smaller and smaller and smaller until the horse was having to tug at it to eat more.

Miss Snow felt the little tug. She jerked her shoe away and looked down.

"Oh! Oh oh oh oh oh! A giant rat! Oh no no no no no!" The words rattled from Miss Snow's mouth. She jumped onto her chair and then clawed her way across the desk. From there she almost fell to the floor, pushed Swan and Bella aside and raced out of the room.

"Quick!" cried Bella. "Get the picture!" Then she dived under Miss Snow's desk and grabbed Astra. She hugged the horse tightly to her chest.

Swan lifted the picture carefully off the wall.

Loud shouts came from the hall as a gang of teachers came towards Miss Snow's room.

"It was a giant rat!" Miss Snow said. "It tried to eat my foot!"

"Don't worry. We'll soon have it!" growled Mr Frost. "Come on everyone!"

"Quick!" cried Bella. "Hurry up!" The voices grew louder, closer and closer.

Swan held the picture steady and slowly began to open the back. Bella stood beside her, holding Astra. As Swan opened the picture frame a smell of the sea filled the room and a breeze plucked at the girls' hair.

"Astra, get inside quickly! Get inside the picture!"

Astra put two hooves inside and sighed. "Rufus!" she breathed. She turned back to the girls. "Thank you," she murmured. Her eyes were shining.

"Just go!" cried Bella. "Hurry!"

Astra stepped into the picture. For a few moments the whole room seemed to fill with wind, sand, sea and sky and a billowing cloak. Then the picture snapped shut, the girls quickly put it back on the wall. They soon had angry teachers all around them.

After that everything was a muddle and a mess. There was a lot of shouting and running about while the teachers went on looking for a rat that wasn't a rat – and not even there any longer!

At last all the noise died down. Miss Snow came back into her office. She looked very nervous. She stared at the picture on the wall. "I thought there was a man in that picture. Hmmm. Very odd, very odd indeed. Odd."

Then Miss Snow looked hard at the two girls. They got a good telling off, but they didn't care. Astra was safe with Rufus. The animal, whatever it had been, wasn't in the school any more and things soon went back to normal.

MISS SNOW
Head Teacher

Swan and Bella walked slowly back to the hall and told the class what had happened. The rest of the class was glad the fuss was over but a bit sad that they no longer had a little white horse to make life exciting for them.

Bella was sorry, too. It had been brilliant fun to have Astra in the house, and at school too. Now she was back on her own again, or was she? Bella suddenly noticed that she was still holding hands with Swan.

Barrington Stoke would like to thank all its readers for commenting on the manuscript before publication and in particular:

Daniel (ISP School)
Humam Alawi
Kevin Allen
Elizabeth Atkinson
Aftab Aziz
Elaine Baker
Aamir Bashir
Marie Belcher
Maaike Bergman
Simon Bounford
Francesca Brodie
Laura Brooker
Chris Butler
Lucrezio Ciotti
Victoria Cistrone
Charlotte Cottrell
Carol DeCoene
Joshua Dobson
Hannah Drews
Charlotte East
Shoana Farman
Daniel Fitt-Palmer
Darren Grocott
Adam Grosvenor
Lysette Harman
Olivier Heinen
Dee Hoult
Anne Hoyle
Jade Hulme
Mehwish Hussain
Margaux Isbecque
Kayleigh James
Magnus Jansåker
Harriet Jeffers
Joseph Kempster
Mehwish Khan
Callan Leavesley
Johan Ljungkuist
Matthew Martin
Amy Massarelle
Amir Mugal
Marguerite Palmer
Joseph Parkin
Shauni Reed
Zafran Shaban
Tayiba Shaffa
Nabeel Siddiq
Nancy Squicciarini
Michelle Starkovs
Halima Tariq
Gina Taylor
Tanita Tipple
Mrs Verner
Luke Walker
Gwen Waller

Become a Consultant!

Would you like to give us feedback on our titles before they are published? Contact us at the email address below – we'd love to hear from you!

Email: info@barringtonstoke.co.uk
Website: www.barringtonstoke.co.uk

If you loved this book, why don't you read ...

Don't Go In the Cellar by Jeremy Strong

Have you ever wanted to go somewhere just because you've been told not to? There is a warning in Zack's bedroom telling him not to go down to the cellar. But when Laura, an unwelcome visitor, comes to stay, they both go exploring – with awful results!

You can order *Don't Go in the Cellar* directly from our website at www.barringtonstoke.co.uk